Robert Quackenbush

I DID IT WITH MY HATCHET

A Story of George Washington

PIPPIN PRESS
NEW YORK

Published by Pippin Press, 229 East 85th Street,
Gracie Station Box #92,
New York, N.Y. 10028

Printed in Spain by Novograph, S.A., Madrid.

10 9 8 7 6 5 4 3 2 1

Library of Congress Cataloging-in-Publication Data

Quackenbush, Robert M.
    I did it with my hatchet.

    Summary: A humorous rendition of George Washington's
life, which includes both famous and little-known
anecdotes.
    1. Washington, George, 1732–1799—Anecdotes—
Juvenile literature.   2. Washington, George, 1732–1799—
Legends.   3. Presidents—United States—Biography—
Juvenile literature.   [1. Washington, George, 1732–1799.
2. Presidents]   I. Title.
E312.66.Q33   1989   973.4'1'0924   [B]   [92]   88-31815
ISBN 0-945912-04-8

For Piet, Margery, & Putty

There was once a boy named George Washington, who was born in Virginia on February 22, 1732. Virginia, in those days, was one of thirteen colonies in America that were all ruled by the British. George's father owned several farms along the Potomac River. One of the smaller farms was called Ferry Farm. George grew up there. He had a younger sister named Elizabeth and three younger brothers named Samuel, John, and Charles. He also had two older half-brothers named Lawrence and Augustine. They were the sons of his father's first wife who had died. Both older brothers attended college in England. But George didn't go away to school and he never went beyond the elementary grades. In his school notebooks he would copy down sayings. One was "Cleanse not your teeth with a tablecloth." Later he made up his own, such as "Better to go laughing than crying through the rough journey of life." But George never said that he chopped down his father's cherry tree with his hatchet. That famous story was made up by Parson Weems for his book *The Life of Washington* published in 1806.

9

When George was eleven, his father died. Lawrence, being the oldest son, received the bulk of the property. This included a large plantation, named Mount Vernon. Soon afterward Lawrence married Anne Fairfax, the daughter of one Virginia's great aristocratic families. Then Mount Vernon became a meeting place for the rich and powerful. George was a frequent visitor. He and Lawrence were very fond of one another. At the plantation George was introduced to a new world that included fox hunts and elegant parties. By age sixteen he was a tall, strapping youth and very much at ease in his new life style. The Fairfaxes were quite impressed by him. He was invited to join a surveying party to divide some of the Fairfax land beyond the Blue Ridge Mountains into farm-size lots. By the time he returned, George had learned a trade. He decided to earn his living as a surveyor.

10

When George was twenty, his brother Lawrence died of tuberculosis and left him Mount Vernon. George had been very close to Lawrence. He wanted to follow in his footsteps. He took over the management of the plantation. Then he set out to fill Lawrence's position as Adjutant General of Virginia. This meant supervising the training of Virginia's military companies. George had no military experience, but gained the position and the rank of Major through the help of Lawrence's friends. Shortly afterward, the French built a fort and became allies with important Indian tribes in the Ohio Valley. This was British territory. Washington volunteered to take a message from the governor of Virginia to the French telling them to abandon the fort. He made the hazardous 1,000-mile journey with guides and interpreters. The news he brought back was not good. The French and Indians were preparing for war to claim the Ohio wilderness.

Three months later Washington led troops into the Ohio Valley. He built a fort in a meadow that was surrounded by high mountains. His plan was to fight the French and Indians in open field combat, like the British military. But the enemy fired from the mountains and drove Washington and what was left of his men from the fort. Then the British sent Major General Edward Braddock and an army of 1,300 men to Washington's aid. Braddock did no better. He would not listen to Washington's warnings to fight in a new way. During the ambush, the general and hundreds of his men were killed. After that the British refused to give Washington further support and moved their troops north. It was left up to Washington to protect the Virginia frontier. The colony provided him with more men, gave him a full colonel's title, and named him Commander in Chief of all Virginia forces. For three long years he kept French and Indian raiders at bay.

15

At last, in November 1758, British forces led by Brigadier General John Forbes returned to the territory. Washington and his Virginia troops joined the British forces and the enemy was driven from the Virginia frontier. Then Washington, at twenty-six, resigned from military life. He returned to Mount Vernon and set out to find a wife. He met Martha Dandridge Custis at a dance. She was a wealthy widow of twenty-seven with two small children named Jacky and Patsy. George courted Martha and they were married at Mount Vernon on January 6, 1759. They were happy together, and the children were happy to have a new, loving father. For the next sixteen years George Washington lived a contented life on his plantation. Martha and he had many visitors. In the evenings, after returning from riding over his farms, George would stay up late with their guests. He enjoyed cracking nuts and listening to rounds of stories and jokes.

In 1763 the nine year French and Indian War finally ended. Great Britain gained almost all of the North American continent. But the war had been expensive. The British taxed the colonies unjustly to help pay the war debt. When the Americans expressed outrage, all but one tax was lifted. The British kept a tax on tea to show their control over the colonies. Late one night, in December 1773, a group of Americans in Boston protested the tax. Dressed as Indians, they boarded three British cargo ships and tossed boxes of tea overboard. As punishment, the British closed the port of Boston and took other harsh measures against the colonies. Soon thereafter, delegates from the colonies met in Philadelphia to form the First Continental Congress. A revolution was brewing. Then, on April 9, 1775, there was bloodshed at Lexington and Concord, outside Boston. The Americans were now ready to raise an army to defend the colonies against British power. Washington suddenly found himself appointed Commanding General and Commander in Chief of the Continental Army.

18

Meanwhile, on June 17, 1775, a major battle took place between British Redcoats and the colonial militia. The battle was staged outside Boston at Breed's Hill (often miscalled Bunker Hill). The Americans lost, but the British forces were severely weakened. On March 4, 1776, Washington took 3,000 of his troops and succeeded in driving the British out of Boston. But he knew that the retreat would not last. Then, on July 4, 1776, the Second Continental Congress signed "The Declaration of Independence." Thomas Jefferson's bold words declared the American colonies "Free and Independent States." The document turned the rebellion into a War of Independence. By July 9th, Washington had taken his army of 23,000 men to defend New York. British ships filled with 30,000 troops arrived in the harbor. After the loss of many men in battle and through desertion, Washington was driven from New York. The city was in flames when he crossed the Hudson River with his army that was now reduced to 7,000 men.

Washington divided what was left of his army. He placed troops along New York's Hudson River to protect the New England colonies from the British. He took the troops that were left—barely 2,400 men—to Philadelphia, the nation's capital. On the night of December 25, 1776, Washington and his ragged and discouraged men crossed the ice-filled Delaware River in barges. His objective was to take Trenton, New Jersey where enemy troops were encamped and sound asleep. The enemy was taken by surprise— 1,000 prisoners were captured as well as hundreds of weapons and a storehouse of supplies. The raid gave the Americans one of the war's most impressive victories. Soon afterward Washington gained another victory at Princeton. Following these successes, the Americans quietly withdrew to Morristown, New Jersey for the winter. Then, the following spring, Washington learned that the British planned to invade Philadelphia. The Americans raced back to the capital.

On October 17, 1777, the Americans defeated 6,000 British troops at Saratoga, New York. But the defeat did not stop other British troops from taking control of Philadelphia. Washington was forced to take his army to Valley Forge, eighteen miles north, to wait out a terrible winter. Many men died of cold, starvation, and disease on that barren plateau. The fate of the American army was being sorely tested during those desperate months. Fortunately, other nations began to recognize America's fight for independence. Baron von Steuben, an expert drillmaster from Prussia, came to help the bedraggled American soldiers. He taught them military drill, the use of bayonets, and other arts of war. He became the army's inspector general. Then came France's Marquis de Lafayette, who at twenty became a brilliant pupil of Washington's. Later he proved to be of great service to the Revolution. But the war dragged on. The Americans suffered defeat after defeat. Finally, on May 12, 1780, the city of Charleston, South Carolina fell to the British.

Charleston was captured by the British General Henry Clinton and his second-in-command, General Charles Cornwallis. After the fall of the city, Clinton returned to New York and left Cornwallis in command of the south. In July 1781, Cornwallis moved the bulk of his forces to Yorktown, Virginia. Then Lafayette persuaded France to send troops, ships, and supplies to aid the revolutionaries. Washington now commanded an army of 17,000 men. He established a battle plan. He set up a phony camp in New Jersey and sent spies to New York. The spies planted rumors that Washington was planning to attack New York so Clinton and his forces would stay put. All was ready. On October 9, 1781 Washington lit the first cannon to start the battle at Yorktown. Cornwallis surrendered in only eight days, on October 17. The battle was not the last military action in the war, but the British were now ready to begin peace talks. A peace treaty was finally signed on September 3, 1783. On December 4, 1783, George Washington held a final meeting with his officers at Fraunces Tavern in New York. He was home by Christmas.

27

In 1787, Washington was asked to preside over a meeting in Philadelphia to draw up a new plan for America's government. Since 1781 the American government had operated under the Articles of Confederation. Better rules of government were needed to unify the states. The new guide—the Constitution of the United States— was signed by fifty-five delegates on September 17, 1787. It gave the federal government new authority including the power to tax, regulate trade, and issue money. It provided for three government branches. The first branch was for a president (the executive branch). The second was for two houses of Congress—the Senate and the House of Representatives (the legislative branch). The third was for a Supreme Court (the judicial branch). A Bill of Rights was also added to the Constitution. These rights included freedom of speech, the press, and religion. After each state approved the Constitution, the next step was to select a president. George Washington was the obvious choice.

On February 4, 1789, George Washington was unanimously elected by the people to serve as the first president of the United States of America. He took his oath of office in the temporary capital of New York City on April 14, 1789. Washington was concerned about what was ahead of him as president. There was much to be done. A huge national debt had to be untangled. An army and navy had to be rebuilt. A new government had to be put on sound footing. To help him were the extraordinarily capable men he had selected for his cabinet. They included Thomas Jefferson as Secretary of State and Alexander Hamilton as Secretary of the Treasury. He set out to discover the needs of his people. He toured the states and made surprise visits to homes and inns along the way. After the tour, he proposed that Congress be made up of members of two political parties, the Republican Party and the Democratic Party. Each party was to have different views to reflect the different needs of the American people.

Washington was elected for a second term and was sworn into office on March 4, 1783. John Adams continued to serve as his vice-president. During this term, Washington had to prove that federal law must be obeyed. He marched an army into western Pennsylvania to stop a rebellion by certain farmers who refused to pay a government tax on whiskey. He also kept the nation out of war during a British-French conflict. By the end of his second term, Washington could see signs of national progress and prosperity. He also saw a city on the Potomac River being laid out just north of Mount Vernon as the new capital, which was to be named after him. However, he refused to consider a third term. He was sixty-five years old when he left the presidency and returned to Mount Vernon.

When Washington returned to Mount Vernon, he found his plantation poorly maintained during the years he had been away. He set to work to have the "wounds" repaired. But during the next two years he was asked to serve his country again. There was a threat of war with France. Washington served as Commander in Chief of the American Army. Fortunately the war did not materialize. Then, at last, he returned to quiet retirement on his plantation. Slaves helped him to maintain Mount Vernon although he also had hired workers. Slavery was a fact of life in Washington's time. But among his deeply felt wishes was a plan by which slavery in America would be abolished by law. For this reason, he made a provision in his will for freeing all the slaves of Mount Vernon after Martha's death.

~Epilogue~

On December 4, 1799, while riding horseback on his plantation in damp weather, George Washington caught cold. His cold developed into pneumonia. Ten days later, on December 14th, he died. America deeply mourned the loss of the father of their country. In the nation's capital, 10,000 people watched as congressmen and government officials led a somber parade through the streets of Philadelphia. The crowd was silent as a great white horse passed them. It carried Washington's saddle and in its stirrups were his boots. The boots had been turned backward to symbolize the death of the horse's master. "All is over now," said Martha Washington. "I shall follow him soon." Three years later, she was buried next to her husband at their beloved Mount Vernon.

36